Dear Parent:
Your child's love of reading starts here!

Every child learns to read in a different way and at his or her own speed. Some go back and forth between reading levels and read favorite books again and again. Others read through each level in order. You can help your young reader improve and become more confident by encouraging his or her own interests and abilities. From books your child reads with you to the first books he or she reads alone, there are I Can Read Books for every stage of reading:

SHARED READING
Basic language, word repetition, and whimsical illustrations, ideal for sharing with your emergent reader

BEGINNING READING
Short sentences, familiar words, and simple concepts for children eager to read on their own

READING WITH HELP
Engaging stories, longer sentences, and language play for developing readers

READING ALONE
Complex plots, challenging vocabulary, and high-interest topics for the independent reader

ADVANCED READING
Short paragraphs, chapters, and exciting themes for the perfect bridge to chapter books

I Can Read Books have introduced children to the joy of reading since 1957. Featuring award-winning authors and illustrators and a fabulous cast of beloved characters, I Can Read Books set the standard for beginning readers.

A lifetime of discovery begins with the magical words "I Can Read!"

*Visit www.icanread.com for information
on enriching your child's reading experience.*

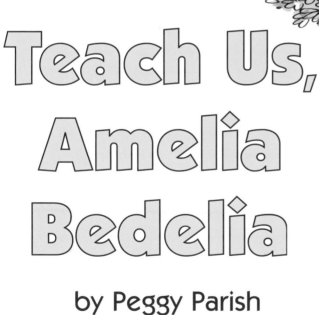

Teach Us, Amelia Bedelia

by Peggy Parish
pictures by Lynn Sweat

HarperCollins*Publishers*

HarperCollins®, 🐻®, and I Can Read Book® are trademarks of HarperCollins Publishers.

Library of Congress Cataloging-in-Publication Data
Parish, Peggy.
  Teach us, Amelia Bedelia / by Peggy Parish ; pictures by Lynn Sweat.
    p.   cm.—(An I can read book)
  "Greenwillow Books."
  Summary: The very literal-minded Amelia Bedelia becomes a substitute teacher for a day.
  ISBN-10: 0-688-80069-6 (trade bdg.) — ISBN-13: 978-0-688-80069-7 (trade bdg.)
  ISBN-10: 0-688-84069-8 (lib. bdg.) — ISBN-13: 978-0-688-84069-3 (lib. bdg.)
  ISBN-10: 0-06-051114-1 (pbk.) — ISBN-13: 978-0-06-051114-2 (pbk.)
  [1. School stories. 2. Teachers—Fiction. 3. Humorous stories.] I. Sweat, Lynn, ill. II. Title.
PZ7.P219 Te   76-22663
[E]   CIP
                                                                                                              AC

❖ Originally published by Greenwillow Books, an imprint of HarperCollins Publishers, in 1977.
                              16 17 SCP 30 29 28

For Miss Rose,
my first-grade teacher,
who introduced me to the magic of words,
with love

The telephone was ringing.

"I'm coming, I'm coming,"

said Amelia Bedelia.

She answered the telephone.

"Mrs. Rogers!" she said.

"Where are you?"

7

"I'm at the airport in Pinewood,"
said Mrs. Rogers.
"You didn't tell me
you were going away,"
said Amelia Bedelia.
"I'm not," said Mrs. Rogers.
"I'm meeting the new teacher.
But her plane is late."
"That's too bad,"
said Amelia Bedelia.

"The telephone at the school

is out of order,"

Mrs. Rogers went on.

"Please go to Mr. Carter's office

at the school. Tell him what I said."

"I'll go right now,"

said Amelia Bedelia.

Amelia Bedelia got her things.

She walked to school.

"Where is Mr. Carter's office?"
she asked.

"That first door," said a child.

Amelia Bedelia walked in.

"Mrs. Rogers tried to call you,"
she said. "But your telephone
is out of order."

"I know," said Mr. Carter.
"But thank goodness you're here.
The children are going wild.
Miss Lane left a list for today.
I'll take you to the room."
He handed Amelia Bedelia the list.

"Follow me," he said.

They went down the hall.

Mr. Carter opened a door.

Children were all over the place.

"All right," said Mr. Carter.

"Quiet! This is your new teacher."

"Me! Teach!" said Amelia Bedelia.

But Mr. Carter was gone.

13

She looked at the children.

They looked at her.

"I'm Amelia Bedelia," she said.

The children giggled.

"You're nice," said Amelia Bedelia.

"I do like happy children.

But we have a lot to do."

She held up the list.

"We must do just what this says,"

she said. "Now, what's first?"

Amelia Bedelia read,

"'Call the roll.'"

She looked puzzled.

"Call the roll! What roll?" she said.

"Does anybody have a roll?"

"I have," said Peter.

"Do get it," said Amelia Bedelia.

Peter opened his lunch box.

"Here it is," he said.

"Now I have to call it,"
said Amelia Bedelia.
"Roll! Hey, roll!
All right, that takes care of that."
The children roared.

Amelia Bedelia read her list.

"For goodness' sake," she said.

"Listen to this.

'Sing a song.'

I never was much of a hand

at singing."

"But it says, sing a song.

So I'll sing."

And she did!

"More! More!" shouted the children.

"No," said Amelia Bedelia.

"It said *a* song. I did just that."

"Aww," said the children.

"Now it's reading time,"
said Amelia Bedelia.
"I know about that.
I read my cookbook.
It tells me just what to do."
She held up a book.
She said, "Is this the right one?"
"Yes," said Amanda.

Amelia Bedelia opened the book.

"I declare," she said.

"This is a good one.

Are you ready?"

"Yes," said the children.

"All right," said Amelia Bedelia.

"It says, 'Run, run, run.'"

The children just sat.

Amelia Bedelia clapped her hands.

"Run," she said. "Run, run, run."

Amelia Bedelia ran.

The children ran after her.

Around the room,

through the halls,

around the block they ran.

Finally they ran

back into the room.

Amelia Bedelia plopped on her chair.

"That takes care of run, run, run,"

she said.

"Your book plumb tired me out.

Let's see what's next.

I hope we don't have to run to do it."

She looked at the list.

She said, "It's science time.

Each of you should plant a bulb.

Do you know about that?"

"Yes," said Tim.

"We brought our pots."

"Where are the bulbs?"

said Amelia Bedelia.

"In the top closet," said Rebecca.

"Miss Lane said so."

Amelia Bedelia looked and looked.

"Nothing here

but some dried-up onions," she said.

"You all go outside.

Put some soil in your pots.

I'll go buy some bulbs."

Amelia Bedelia went to the store.

She hurried back.

The children were waiting.

"Here's a bulb for you and you,"

said Amelia Bedelia.

She gave everybody a bulb.

The children looked surprised.

Then they started giggling.

But they planted those bulbs.

They put the pots on the window sill.

"Those do look right pretty,"

said Amelia Bedelia.

"And I learned something new.

I didn't know you could plant bulbs."

30

Suddenly a bell rang.

"What's that for?"

said Amelia Bedelia.

"Free time," yelled the children.

"Good," said Amelia Bedelia.

The children ran outside.

Amelia Bedelia sat down to rest.

Then free time ended.

Back came the children.

"It's quiet time now,"

said Amelia Bedelia.

"You're supposed to read stories."

Each child chose a book.

All was quiet.

"Why aren't you reading?"

said Amelia Bedelia.

"We are,"

said Ed.

"I don't hear you," said Amelia Bedelia.

The children looked at Amelia Bedelia.

They looked at each other.

And Amelia Bedelia heard them

all right. "My, I'll be glad

when quiet time is over," she said.

"My ears hurt."

Jeff said, "Art comes next.

That's fun."

Amelia Bedelia looked at her list.

"You're right," she said.

"You must paint pictures now."

The children got sheets of art paper.

"What are you doing?"
said Amelia Bedelia.
"We're going
to paint pictures," said Bud.
"But how can you?"
said Amelia Bedelia.
"There's no picture there to paint."
"We'll make pictures," said Mary.
"Oh no!" said Amelia Bedelia.
"This says to paint pictures.
You can't paint a picture
without a picture to paint.
Better find one for yourselves."

The children ran around the room.

Not a picture was left on the wall.

But all the children were painting.

Soon the pictures were back

on the wall.

"They sure look different," said Steve.

"Yes," said Amelia Bedelia.

"Mr. Carter will be surprised."

The children shook their heads.

"He sure will," said Janet.

"What's next?" said Jamie.

"Our play," said Rebecca.

"We have to practice our play."

"Practice play!" said Amelia Bedelia.

"You mean children

have to practice play?

School sure has changed since I went.

All right, out you go."

"But Amelia Bedelia,"

said the children.

"No buts," said Amelia Bedelia.

"Let's go. Start playing."

"Practice that jumping rope
some more," said Amelia Bedelia.
"I can do better than that."
"Show us," said Janet.
And Amelia Bedelia did.

"I can run faster than that,"
said Amelia Bedelia.
"Show us," said Steve.
So Amelia Bedelia did.

"That's fine," she said.
"You've practiced long enough.
Let's go inside."

"Let me see what's next,"

said Amelia Bedelia.

"Here are some problems for you."

"Yuck!" said the children.

"Ginny, get your apples,"

said Amelia Bedelia.

"What apples?" said Ginny.

Amelia Bedelia looked puzzled.

She said, "But it says

Ginny has four apples.

Paul takes away two."

"Oops," said Amelia Bedelia.
"I don't think I was
supposed to tell that part."
She read the other problems.
"These all have apples in them,"
she said.
"Does anybody have apples?"
The children shook their heads.

Then Amelia Bedelia had an idea.

"Let's go to my house," she said.

"We have lots of apples."

"Yes!" shouted the children.

"We better leave a note,"

said Amelia Bedelia.

She went to the blackboard

and wrote,

Then off they went

to the Rogers' backyard.

Amelia Bedelia got the apples.

She called some children.

"There is a problem

for each of you," she said.

"You all have apples.

Somebody is going to try

to take some away.

Are you going to let them?"

"No!" shouted the children.

Amelia Bedelia went
to the other children.
"You are supposed to take away
some of their apples," she said.
She told each child
whom to take from.
"Can you do that?" she said.
"Sure!" said the children.

"All right, everybody,"
said Amelia Bedelia. "Go!"
Children started after each other.
They ran all over the yard.

Amelia Bedelia turned

and went into the kitchen.

She put some of this and

a lot of that into a big pot.

She put the pot on the stove.

"There," she said.

"I'll surprise them."

Amelia Bedelia started out.

Just then Mr. Rogers started in.

"What is all of this?" said Mr. Rogers.

"What are those children doing?"

"Math," said Amelia Bedelia.

"Math!" said Mr. Rogers.

"Come see," said Amelia Bedelia.

They went out.

"That's not fair, Steve,"
yelled Janet. "You hid your apples.
I can't take any."

"That's not fair, Judy,"
shouted Andy.

"You took away all my apples."

"What in tarnation are they doing?"

said Mr. Rogers.

Amelia Bedelia read him

the problems.

"That sounds like fun.

I'm going to help them," he said.

He joined the children.

"Now that does beat all,"

said Amelia Bedelia.

She went inside.

Later she called,

"Everybody come.

All apples on the table."

Apples came from everywhere.

Amelia Bedelia put a stick

in each one.

Then she dipped them in the pot.

"Taffy apples!" everybody shouted.

"Right," said Amelia Bedelia.

"Take one and go home.

School is out."

The children grabbed apples.

They crowded around Amelia Bedelia.

"Please, please teach us again,"

each one said.

Amelia Bedelia said nothing.

She looked at her kitchen

and shook her head.

Mrs. Rogers walked in.

Someone was with her.

"What happened?" she said.

"Where are the children?"

"Home," said Amelia Bedelia.

"Home!" said Mrs. Rogers.

"But it's not time."

"It was for me,"

said Amelia Bedelia.

"This is Miss Reed," said Mrs. Rogers.

"She is the new teacher.

She came to get the children."

"Then she will have to find them,"

said Amelia Bedelia.

"I'm plumb tired out."

"But, but . . ." said Miss Reed.

"More taffy apples," called Mr. Rogers.

"Taffy apples!" said Mrs. Rogers.

"Come on, Miss Reed."

Amelia Bedelia put the taffy apples

on the table.

They all sat down and ate.

"I'll let you teach anytime,"
said Miss Reed,
"if you will make taffy apples."
"Be glad to," said Amelia Bedelia.
"I do love children."

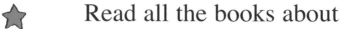

Read all the books about

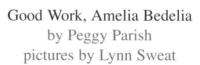
Amelia Bedelia

Amelia Bedelia Goes Camping
by Peggy Parish
pictures by Lynn Sweat

Merry Christmas, Amelia Bedelia
by Peggy Parish
pictures by Lynn Sweat

Amelia Bedelia's Family Album
by Peggy Parish
pictures by Lynn Sweat

Good Driving, Amelia Bedelia
by Herman Parish
pictures by Lynn Sweat

Bravo, Amelia Bedelia!
by Herman Parish
pictures by Lynn Sweat

Amelia Bedelia 4 Mayor
by Herman Parish
pictures by Lynn Sweat

Calling Doctor Amelia Bedelia
by Herman Parish
pictures by Lynn Sweat

Amelia Bedelia, Bookworm
by Herman Parish
pictures by Lynn Sweat

Happy Haunting, Amelia Bedelia
by Herman Parish
pictures by Lynn Sweat

Amelia Bedelia, Rocket Scientist?
by Herman Parish
pictures by Lynn Sweat

Amelia Bedelia Under Construction
by Herman Parish
pictures by Lynn Sweat

Peggy Parish

was the author of many books enjoyed by children of all ages. Among her easy-to-read books are a number of beloved books about Amelia Bedelia. Originally from Manning, South Carolina, Peggy Parish taught school in Texas, Oklahoma, Kentucky, and New York.

Lynn Sweat

has illustrated many Amelia Bedelia books, including *Bravo, Amelia Bedelia!*; *Good Driving, Amelia Bedelia*; *Amelia Bedelia and the Baby*, and *Amelia Bedelia, Rocket Scientist?* He is a painter as well as an illustrator, and his paintings hang in galleries across the country. He and his wife live in Connecticut.